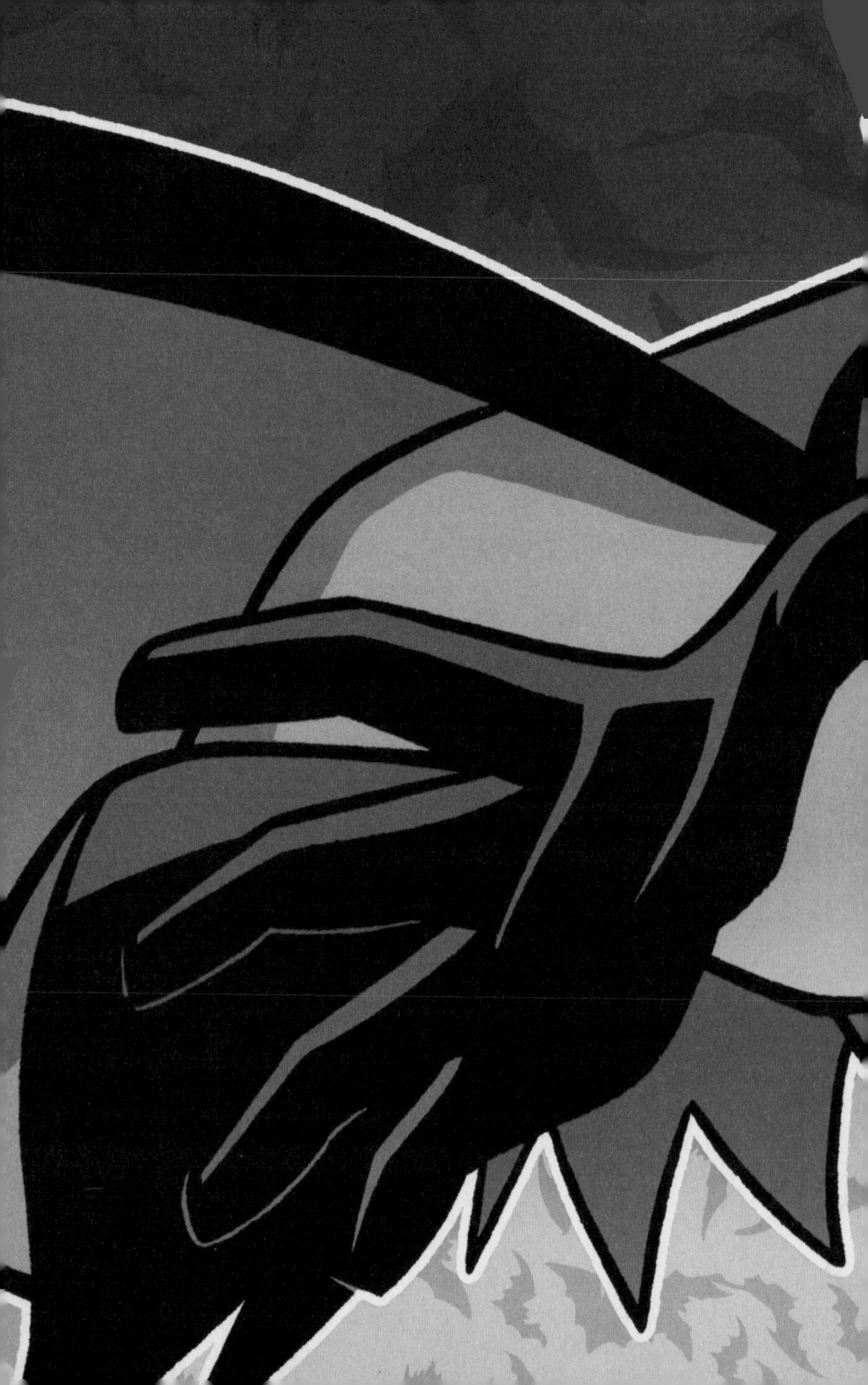

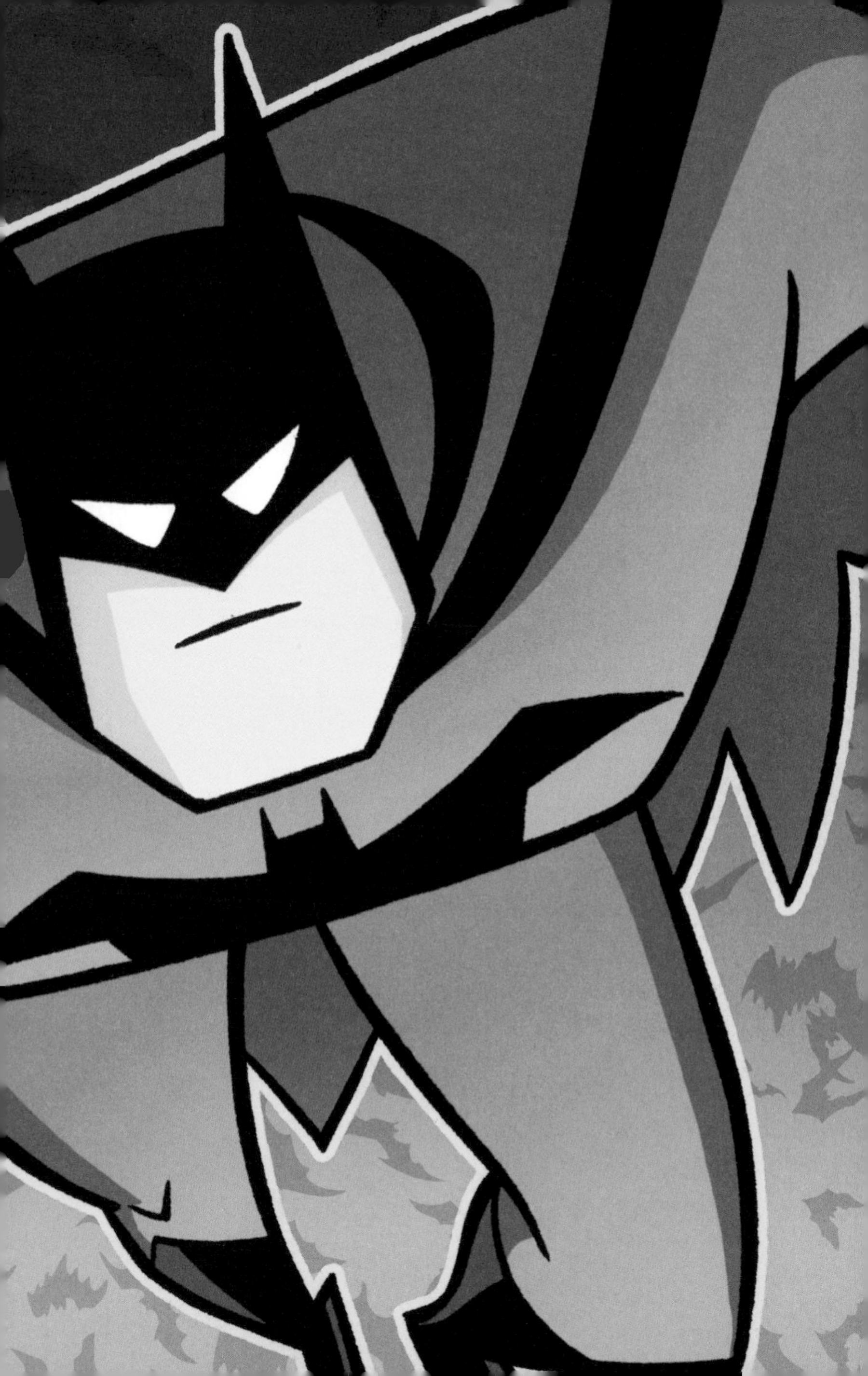

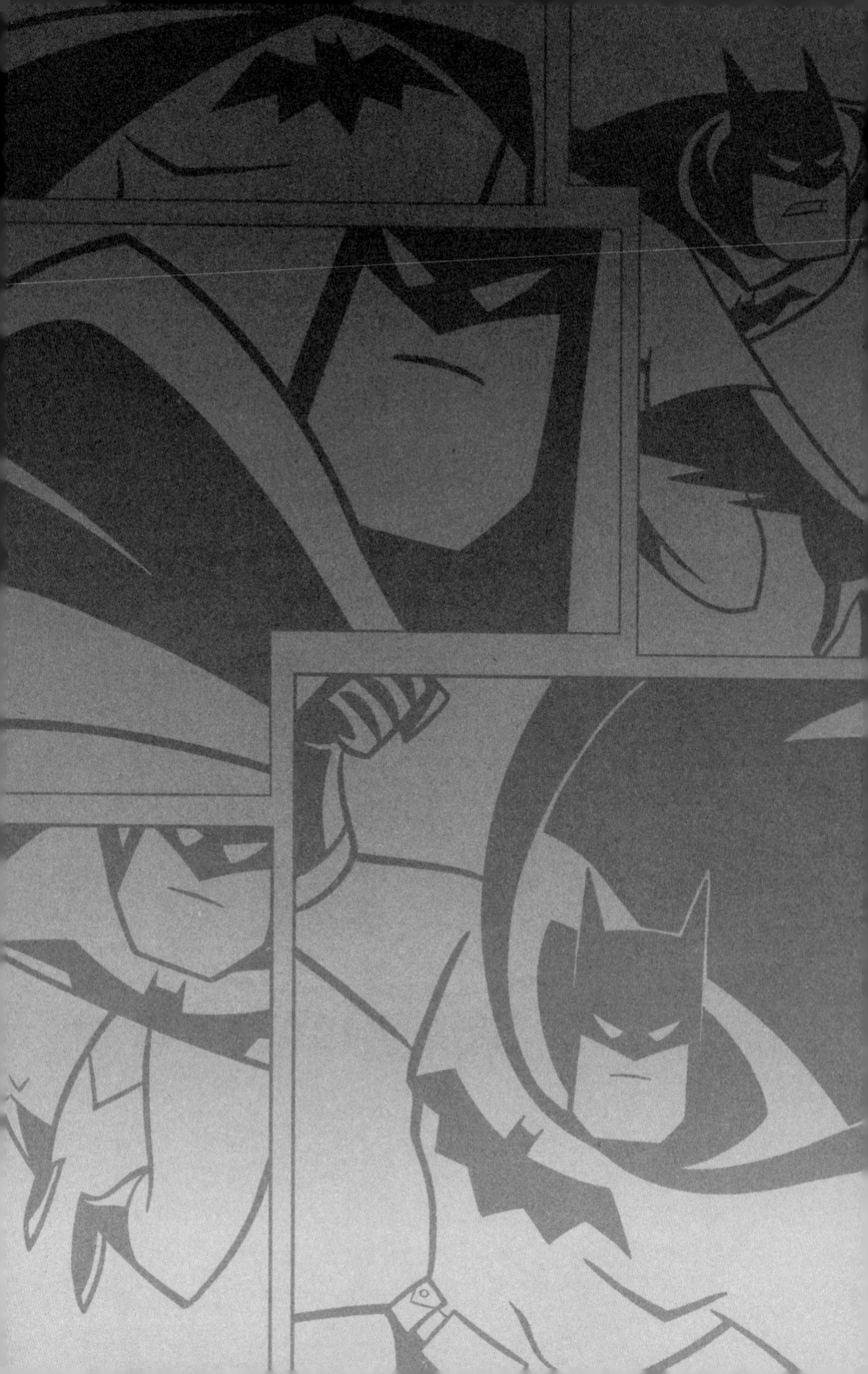

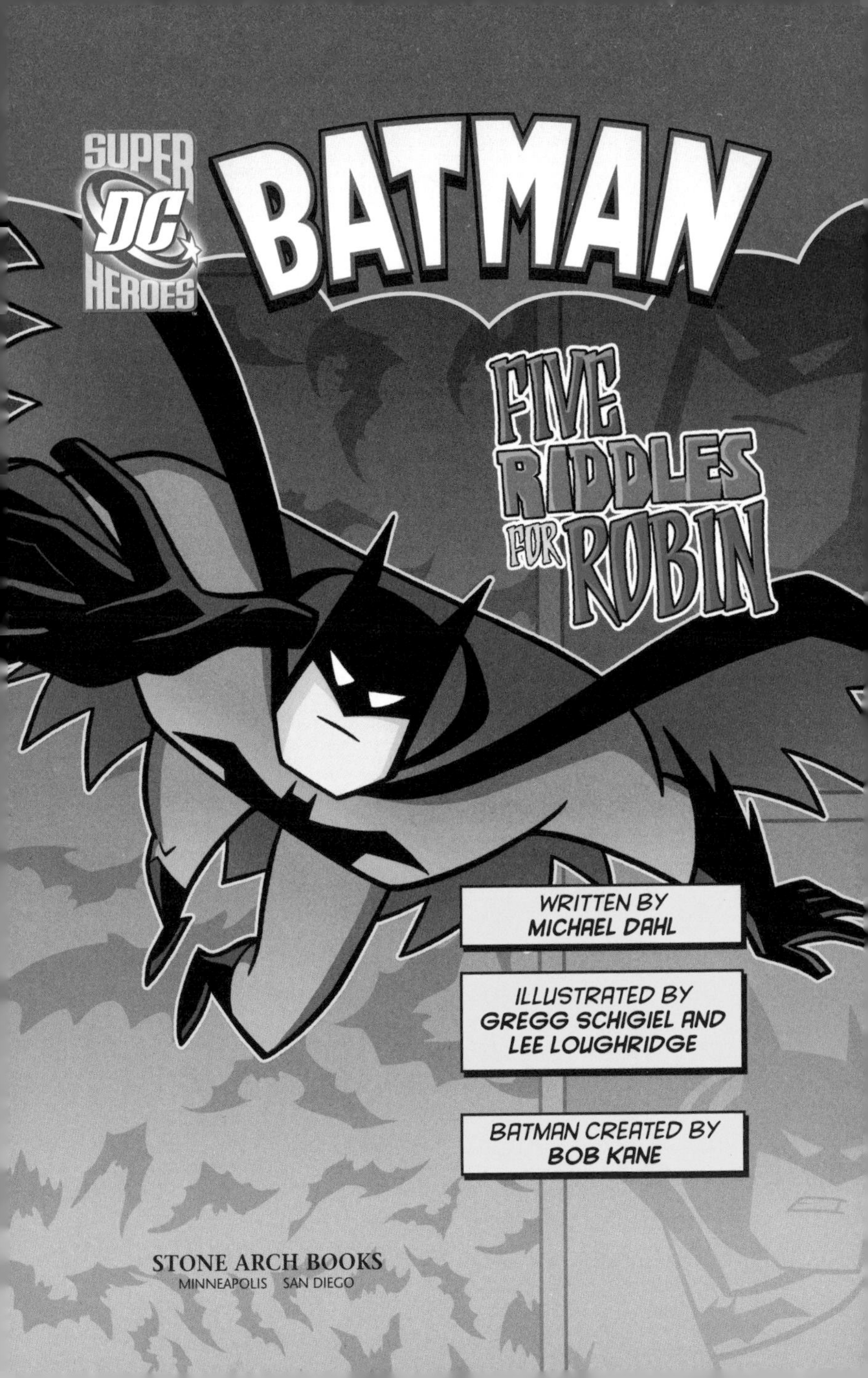
SUPER DC HEROES
BATMAN
FIVE RIDDLES FOR ROBIN
WRITTEN BY
MICHAEL DAHL
ILLUSTRATED BY
GREGG SCHIGIEL AND
LEE LOUGHRIDGE
BATMAN CREATED BY
BOB KANE
STONE ARCH BOOKS
MINNEAPOLIS SAN DIEGO

Published by Stone Arch Books in 2009
151 Good Counsel Drive, P.O. Box 669
Mankato, Minnesota 56002
*www.stonearchbooks.com*



*Library of Congress Cataloging-in-Publication Data*
Dahl, Michael.
Five Riddles for Robin / by Michael Dahl; illustrated by Gregg Schigiel.
p. cm. — (DC Super Heroes. Batman)
ISBN 978-1-4342-1151-4 (library binding)
ISBN 978-1-4342-1366-2 (pbk.)
[1. Superheroes—Fiction.] I. Schigiel, Gregg, ill. II. Title.
PZ7.D15134Fi 2009
[Fic]—dc22 2008032402

Summary: Batman has been kidnapped by the Riddler! The crook has left behind one of his infamous riddles, addressed to Robin. If Robin can solve the puzzle, he will locate the Caped Crusader. But that first riddle leads to another. Then the Riddler turns off all the lights in Gotham City. What, Robin wonders, is the point? When will the riddles end? If the Boy Wonder cannot find his partner by the next sunrise, Batman will be gone forever.

Art Director: Bob Lentz
Designer: Brann Garvey

1 2 3 4 5 6 14 13 12 11 10 09

Printed in the United States of America

# TABLE OF CONTENTS



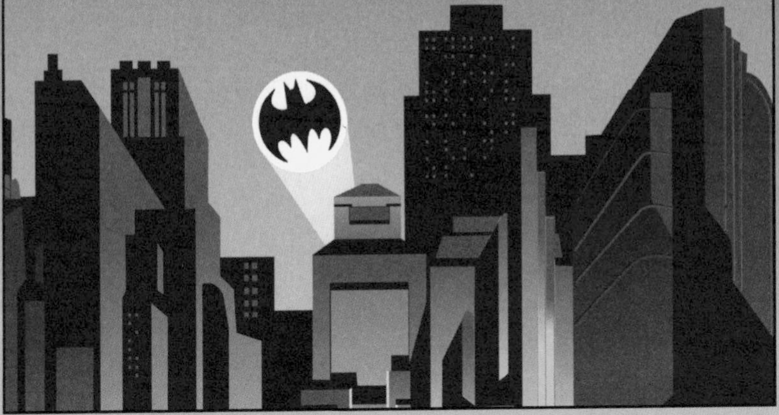

# CHAPTER 1

# THE FIRST RIDDLE

School was over for the day at Gotham Junior High School. The students and teachers had gone home. But the lights were still on inside the gymnasium. One young athlete stayed late to practice.

Tim Drake dusted his hands with chalk. Then he pulled out a long black piece of cloth from his gym bag. He tied it around his eyes like a blindfold.

"Let's do this the fun way," he said.

Tim jumped up, grabbing the high bar.

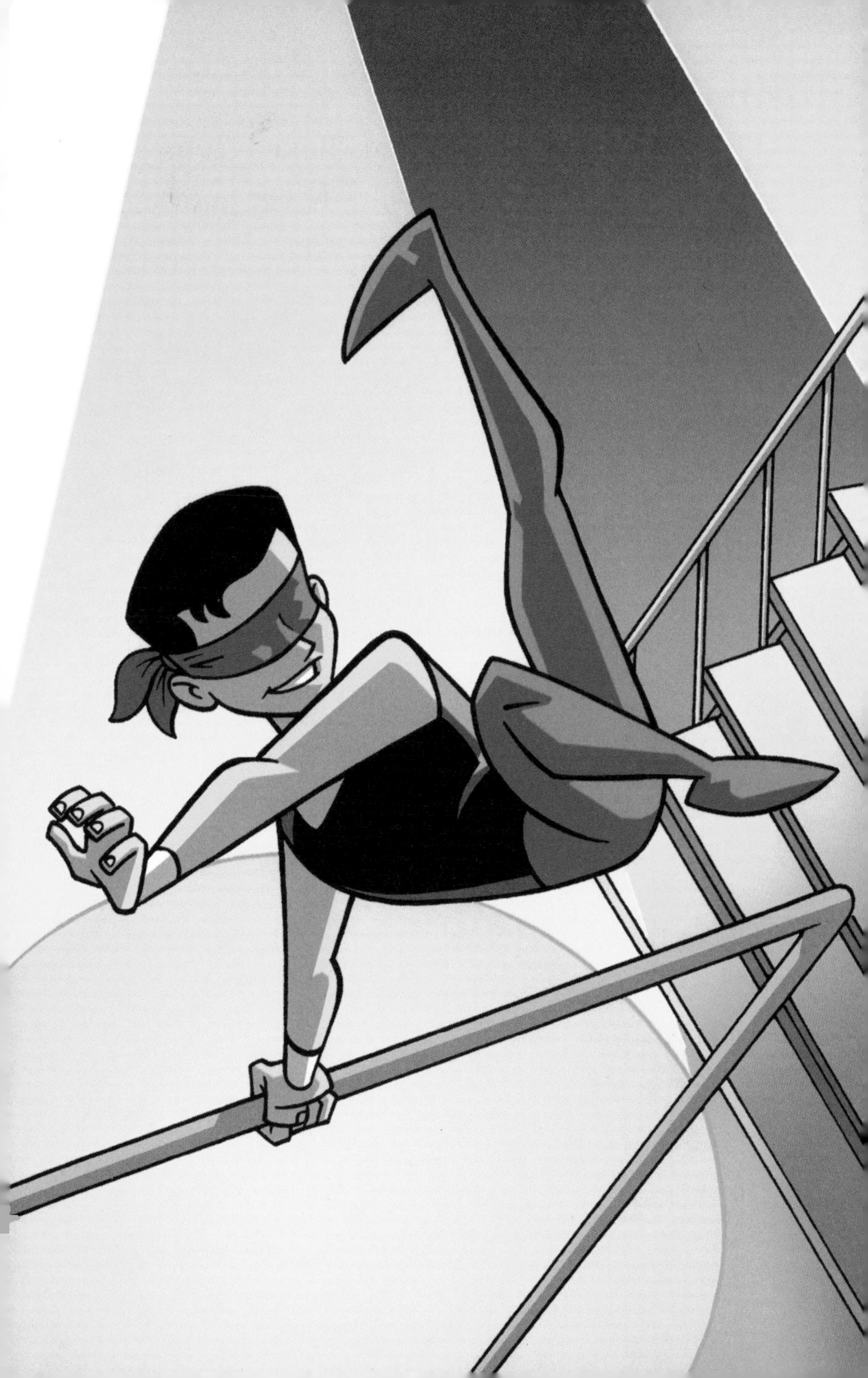

The muscles in his arms flexed as he gripped the bar. Tim swung back and forth. Soon he was whirling completely around the bar.

Tim flipped, he jumped, and he changed direction. For several minutes, he practiced his moves, swinging through the air.

Suddenly, he let go of the bar. He somersaulted twice and then landed on the mat, feet together, arms up. The perfect dismount. Throughout the practice, Tim had not been able to see a thing through his blindfold.

"Who needs to see?" Tim said to himself. "I'm better than a bat in the dark!"

Tim's cell phone buzzed inside of his gym bag.

"Great timing," said Tim. He smiled to himself. He ripped off his blindfold.

When he picked up his phone, Tim's smile turned to a frown. A text message covered the screen:

BATMAN KIDNAPPED! CALL ME!

Tim punched in a number.

"Alfred," he said. "What happened to Bruce?"

Bruce Wayne was Tim's friend and mentor. He was also Batman, Gotham City's greatest hero. Only Tim Drake and Alfred Pennyworth, the Wayne family butler, knew of Batman's secret identity.

Tim was sure that Alfred had made a mistake. How could Batman, the powerful Dark Knight, be kidnapped?

Alfred's voice was filled with worry.

"I'm not sure how it happened," he said. "Master Bruce left an hour ago. He saw the Bat-Signal shining over the city. He knew there was trouble. Then Batman heard a message on the police scanner that a diamond store was being robbed. That's the last I heard from him," added Alfred.

"How do you know he was kidnapped?" asked Tim.

"The police received a message a few minutes ago," replied Alfred. "The sender said he had captured Batman and he had a message for Robin."

"For me?" cried Tim.

Alfred took a deep breath. "Yes, it was a riddle. It goes, How is a baseball field like a wealthy woman?"

"This is bad," said Tim. "This is really bad. That riddle means that Batman's kidnapper is the Riddler!"

"I'm afraid so," agreed Alfred. "Can you solve the riddle, Master Tim? Do you think the Riddler plans to rob some poor woman during a baseball game?"

Tim shook his head. The Riddler was one of his and Batman's cleverest enemies. He was a genius who once used his amazing brain to build the world's greatest computer games. Then his plans backfired. So he turned to evil.

The Riddler loved to trick and torment Batman. He always gave riddles as clues to what he was planning next. The villain thought no one would be smart enough to figure them out. So far, Batman and Robin had proven him wrong.

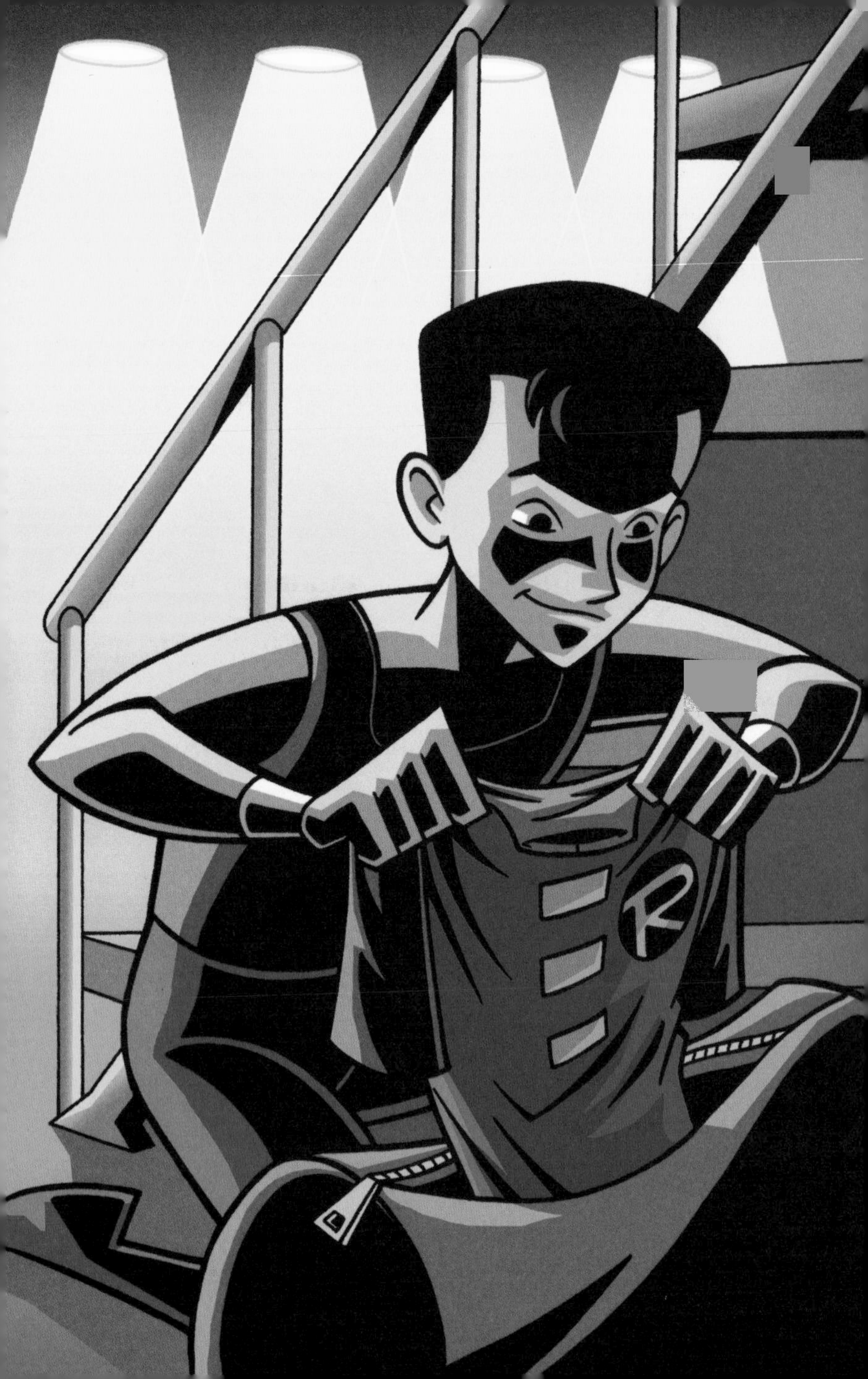

Tim wondered. Would he be able to solve the Riddler's puzzle by himself?

The young athlete zipped opened a secret pocket in his gym bag. He made sure his Robin uniform was tucked safely inside. He needed to make a quick change before the school engineer returned to turn out the gym lights.

Lights, he thought. Like lights at a baseball game, shining down on the field. On the diamond. That was it!

"The answer is diamonds," said Tim. "Baseball fields and rich women both have diamonds."

# CHAPTER 2

# THE RIDDLER'S CHALLENGE

An hour later, a masked figure appeared in the doorway of the Deluxe Diamond store. It was Robin, the Boy Wonder.

"Robin!" The store security guard recognized the young hero at once. "What are you doing here? The robbers and Batman are already gone. I think your partner scared them off."

Robin frowned. The guard must not have heard about the message sent to the police. He did not know yet that Gotham City's hero had been kidnapped.

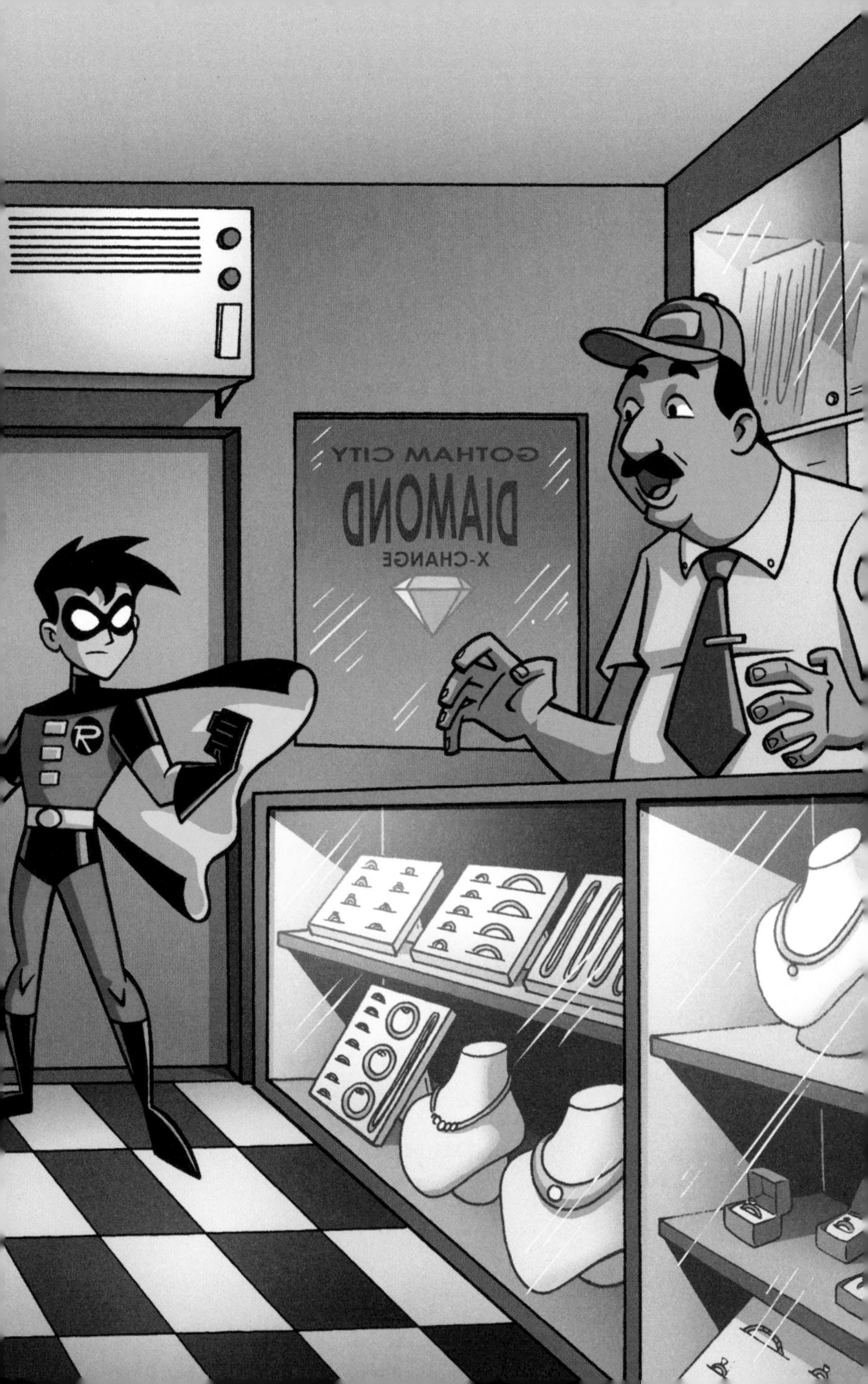
GOTHAM CITY
DIAMOND
X-CHANGE

"Uh, yes," said Robin. "Batman sent me to check something out for him."

"Everything's fine now," said the guard. "The crooks didn't get away with any diamonds."

"That's good." The teenager read the man's name tag: Miller.

"Well, Mr. Miller," added Robin. "The crooks may be gone, but I think they may have left something behind. Have you checked your security camera's tapes yet?"

"No, Robin," said Miller. "I didn't think we needed to." The guard explained that Batman had stopped the robbery. The store manager wasn't worried about checking the cameras.

"As soon as Batman got here, he told me to wait outside," said Miller.

Miller pointed to the spot he had hidden. "A half hour later, I noticed it was quiet," he continued. "That's when I went back in and saw everyone was gone."

Miller led Robin into the security office at the back of the building. Inside, they played the video from the time of the robbery.

"I knew it!" exclaimed Robin. "It is the Riddler!"

The video showed a tall, thin man entering the store. He wore a green costume. A huge purple question mark covered his chest.

"I've heard of the Riddler before," said the guard. "But I've never seen him up close. He must have come in through the back."

"Take it from me," said Robin. "You don't want to get anywhere near that creep. He's bad news."

The Riddler didn't seem to be interested in the store's diamonds. He was just standing there. Waiting. An evil smile was on his lips.

As Robin and Miller watched the video, they saw the moment when Batman arrived at the store. His dark shape swooped into view, confronting the lanky villain. The Riddler raised his cane, which was shaped like a question mark.

"What's he doing? asked Miller.

Robin knew that the deadly cane was one of the Riddler's weapons. It could send out a painful stream of electricity. But this time, there was no flash. No zap.

Instead, a cloud of purple smoke spurted at the Dark Knight. Batman fell to the floor.

Robin cried out, even though he knew he was only looking at a recording.

"Knockout gas," said Miller. "That guy is dangerous."

The Riddler laughed. Then he stared directly at the video camera. "I hope you're watching this, Boy Blunder," said the Riddler. "Batman and I are far away by now. We're enjoying some quiet, quality time. But I'd love for you to join us."

Robin clenched his hands in anger.

Then the Riddler held a piece of paper up to the camera.

"Here's your invitation, punk," came the Riddler's voice.

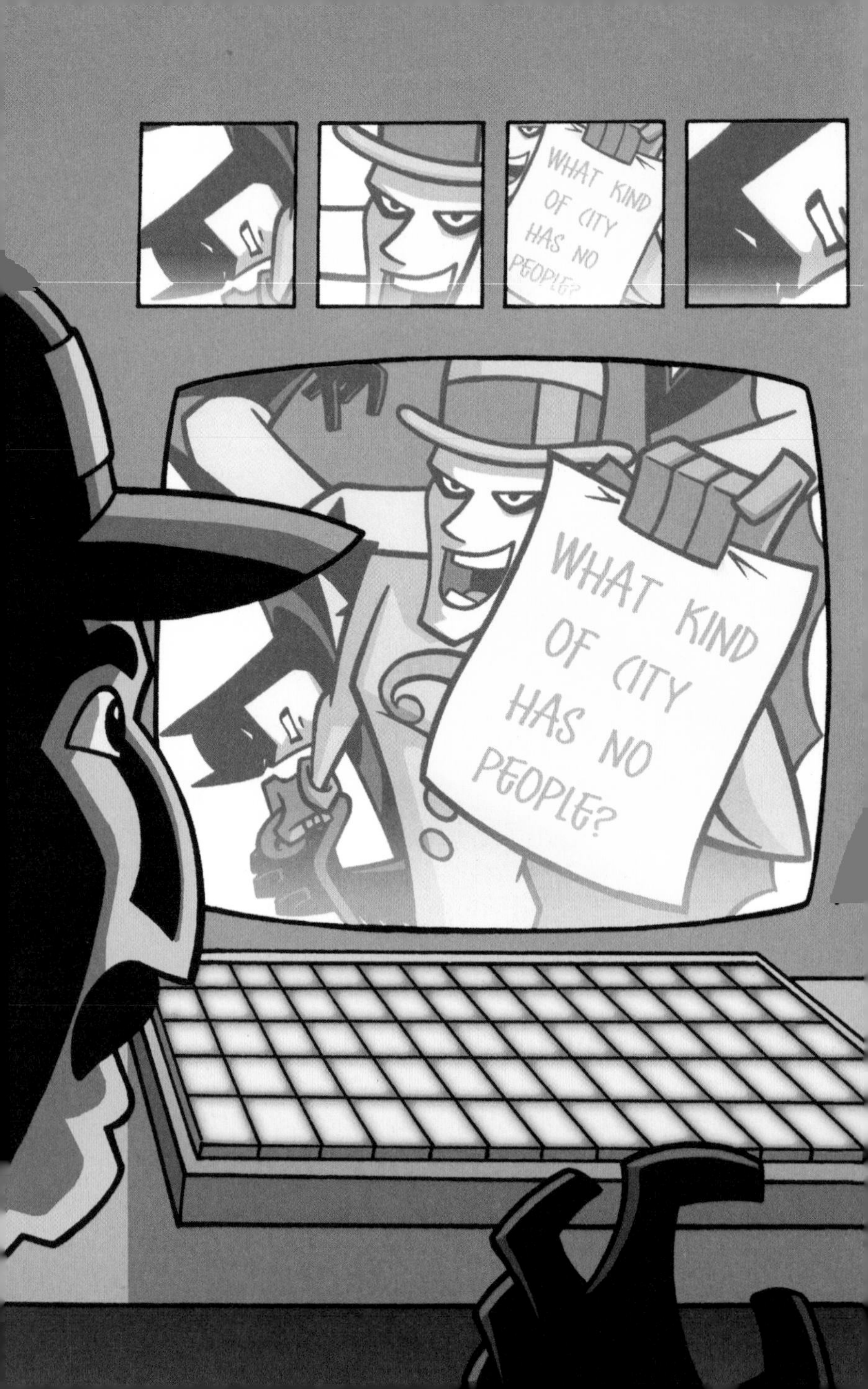

WHAT KIND OF CITY HAS NO PEOPLE?
WHAT KIND OF CITY HAS NO PEOPLE?

"What does that mean?" asked the guard.

"Solve the puzzle, if you can," said the Riddler. "Your partner's life depends on it. If you can't solve the puzzle before sunrise, the Dark Knight will never wake up!"

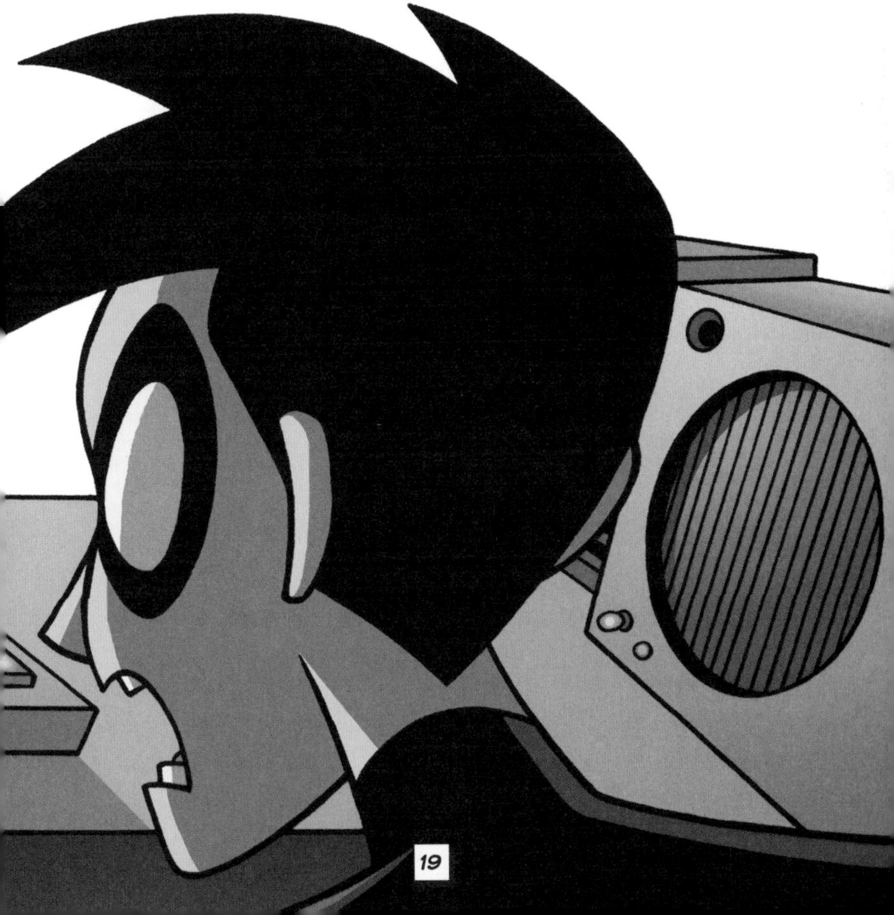

# THE BAT-SIGNAL

"The Riddler has Batman?" asked the stunned security guard.

"I need you to keep this a secret, Mr. Miller," said Robin. "I don't want other criminals to know about this. We could have a crime wave on our hands."

The guard nodded. "But what will you do?" he asked.

Batman could be anywhere, thought Robin. Gotham City had hundreds of city blocks. It had thousands of buildings.

"I'm going for backup," said Robin.

"Can you solve that riddle, Robin?"

The boy smiled grimly. "I'll have to, won't I?" Then he raced out of the room.

In a dark alley near the diamond store, Robin had hidden his Redbird motorcycle. A few seconds later, the turbo-charged racer was rushing through the streets of Gotham City.

ZWWWOOOMMMMM!

Batman had been missing for more than an hour, thought Robin. He might not even be in Gotham City anymore. Some backup might help. Maybe Police Commissioner Gordon could spare some extra officers for the search. They would hunt all night if they had to.

"What kind of city has no people?" Robin said to himself. "An empty city? Gotham City at night? A lost city?"

Robin was trying to come up with the answer to the puzzle. He wasn't prepared for the Riddler's next trick. Just as his cycle was racing toward police headquarters, and crossing busy Gotham Square, the lights of the city went out. Every skyscraper, every office window, every store sign went black. Only the headlights of cars and taxis and the Redbird remained. The rest of the city was plunged into complete darkness.

Cars and taxis crashed into each other. Horns honked. All the city's traffic lights had gone out, too. Police officers ran to the scenes of dozens of accidents.

"I'll bet the Riddler is behind this, too," said Robin. His cycle zipped in and out of groups of confused pedestrians.

"Whoa!" said a teenage boy, standing on a street corner. "That was Robin!"

"Maybe he knows who turned off the electricity," yelled the boy's friend.

"That's it!" Robin said. "Electricity. What city has no people? Electri-city! But why did the Riddler turn off the juice?"

The towering office buildings looked like giant mountains in the darkness. A bright, white light shined suddenly above them. The round white shape was reflected on the clouds.

"It's the Bat-Signal," cried Robin. "Something else is going down."

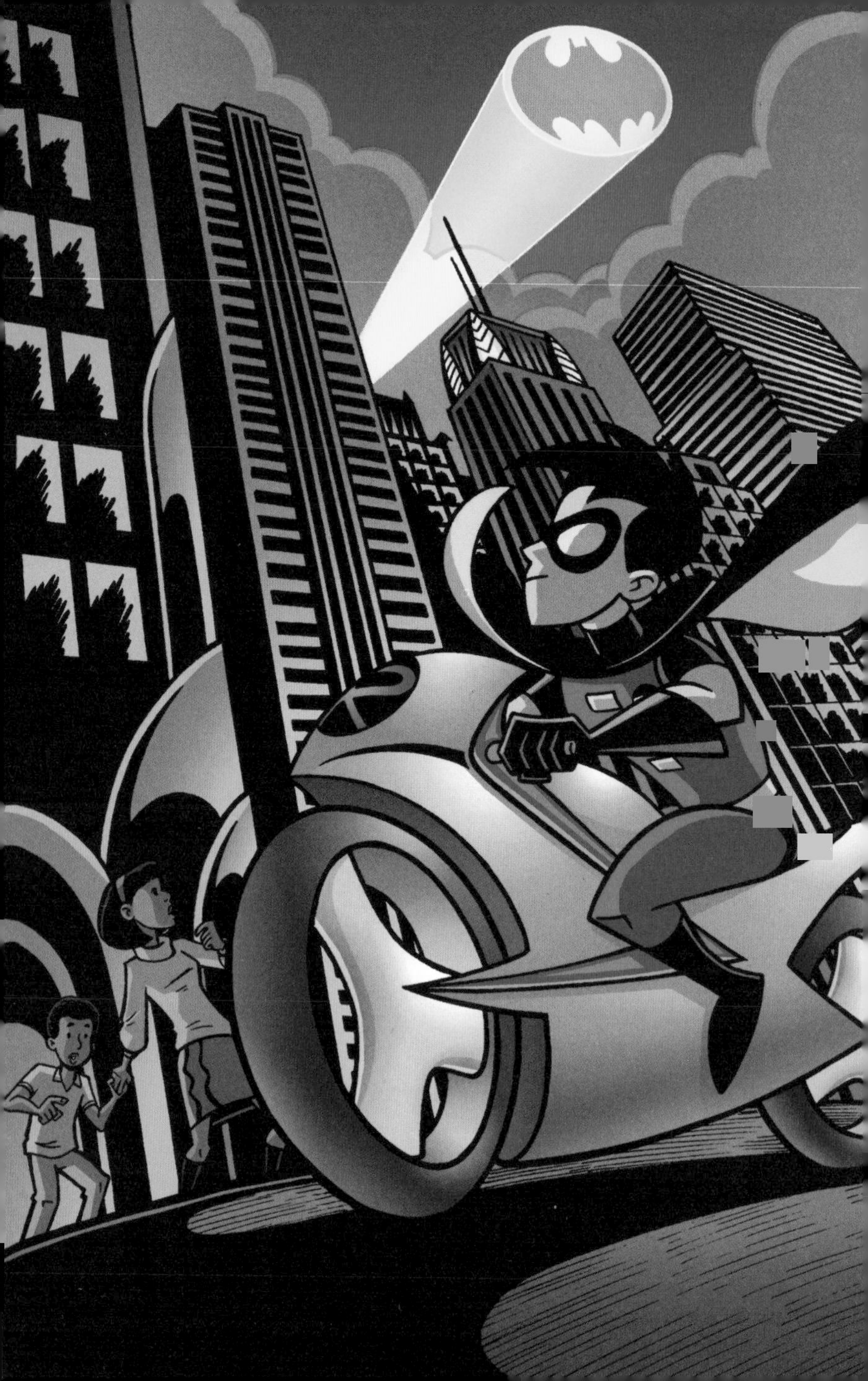

Robin turned on his belt radio. He wanted to listen to any police reports of criminal activity. The Bat-Signal was always a sign that the police needed Batman and Robin's special help.

Robin adjusted the radio controls with one hand. He steered the rocketing cycle with the other.

"10-33," came the radio. It was a police scanner alert. "10-33, a robbery in progress. At Lite Foods Warehouse on the docks."

Robin lowered his head. He gripped the brake controls on the handle. The Redbird screeched and slid into a U-turn.

Then the teenager gunned the engine and roared toward Gotham Harbor.

VROOOOM!!

The docks along the harbor were as dark as the rest of the city. A few dim lights from freighters and tugboats twinkled on the water. The cycle's powerful headlamp lighted up the wooden platforms and warehouse doors. Robin saw a sign: Lite Foods Warehouse.

The Redbird skidded to a stop.

"Funny," said Robin quietly. "No one's around."

The young hero carefully walked up to the building. The windows were dark. The door was locked. Was this a trap set by the Riddler?

A ship's deep whistle broke the silence. Robin glanced up and down the docks.

"This place is dead," he said to himself. "No break-in. No crooks. How could the police radio be wrong?"

# CHAPTER 4

# MIXED SIGNALS

For more than an hour, Robin searched along the docks. He was completely alone. Then above the blacked-out buildings, Robin saw the Bat-Signal shine again.

"What's going on?" he said.

The radio burst on. Then Robin heard a familiar voice. "This message is for your ears only, Boy Wonder. What building has the most stories?"

Robin was startled. He pressed the Send button on his belt radio.

"Riddler, is that you? Where's Batman?" he demanded.

An awful laugh sounded on the radio. "Chin up, kid," came the Riddler's voice. "I know you'll see the light soon."

"Batman, are you there?" shouted Robin into the radio. "Can you hear me?"

"He can hear you," said the villain. "He just can't answer. So save your breath and solve the riddle. It will lead you right to the Caped Crusader. I just hope you're in time!"

"Riddler, why did you turn off the electricity?" said Robin. "What's going on?"

The radio went dead.

"Darn!" said Robin. "If he'd stayed on the radio longer, I would have been able to figure out his location. Maybe I can find the signal from Batman's Utility Belt."

Robin tried several buttons on his belt. It was no use. The Riddler must have found the homing signal on Batman's Utility Belt and turned it off.

Robin returned to his cycle. He sat down and took a deep breath. Things were not looking good. If Batman was without his Utility Belt, then he really was in deep trouble. The Riddler wasn't just boasting.

Robin checked the time. It was almost midnight. Sunrise would come before six o'clock. That meant he had less than five hours to find Batman.

He must find him!

The answer to the third riddle was easy. "It's an old one," Robin said to himself. He zoomed away from the docks. "The library is the building with the most stories."

Once more the turbo-charged Redbird rocketed through the streets. When Robin arrived at the Gotham City Library, the city's power was still out. The huge stone building was dark.

Robin switched on his flashlight. Tall stone pillars stood at the top of a flight of steps. On either crouched a massive stone lion. Robin ignored the statues. His attention was drawn to the marble steps.

"Riddle number four," said Robin.

Across the white stone steps, a message had been spray-painted:

WHAT FALLS BUT NEVER BREAKS?
THAT'S THE TIME THE
BATMAN BAKES!

Robin switched off his flashlight and stood in the dark.

"Think, Robin, think," he told himself. "How do all these riddles add up? When are they going to lead me to Batman?"

As if in answer to his question, a light blinked on high above him. The Bat-Signal blazed above the dark skyscrapers. From the steps of the library, Robin had his clearest view so far of the signal's light.

The teenager rolled his eyes. "Right. I'm not falling for that one again. The Bat-Signal was wrong about that last break-in. Somehow the Riddler used a fake signal."

Suddenly, the lights went on in Robin's brain. "That's it!" he cried. "The Bat-Signal lured Batman to the diamond store where he was captured."

"The Bat-Signal lured me to a fake robbery by the docks," Robin added. "The lights went out so that the only real light in the city is the Bat-Signal. But, if all the power is out, why is the signal still on? Because it's a fake signal!"

Robin switched on his flashlight once more and stared at the riddle painted on the steps.

## WHAT FALLS BUT NEVER BREAKS?

"The answer is night," said Robin. "Night falls, but it doesn't really break."

Then Robin realized that the clever Riddler was doing everything at night so that Robin could not miss seeing the Bat-Signal. Robin pulled a set of binoculars from the Redbird. The lenses zoomed in on the Bat-Signal.

"It's not coming from the top of police headquarters," said Robin. "I knew it! It's not the real signal at all. That must be where the Riddler is keeping Batman!"

Robin pulled a climbing device from his belt. He held the grapnel in his fist, aimed, and fired. The device shot a metal dart at the building across the street from the Gotham Library. As the dart flew, it spun out a line of super-strong wire behind it.

Ka-Pannng! The dart dug into the concrete wall of the building. It made a strong anchor for Robin's next move.

The young athlete held onto the grappling device and pressed the Rewind button. Zing! The device swiftly pulled on the steel wire. It yanked Robin across the street and onto the side of the building.

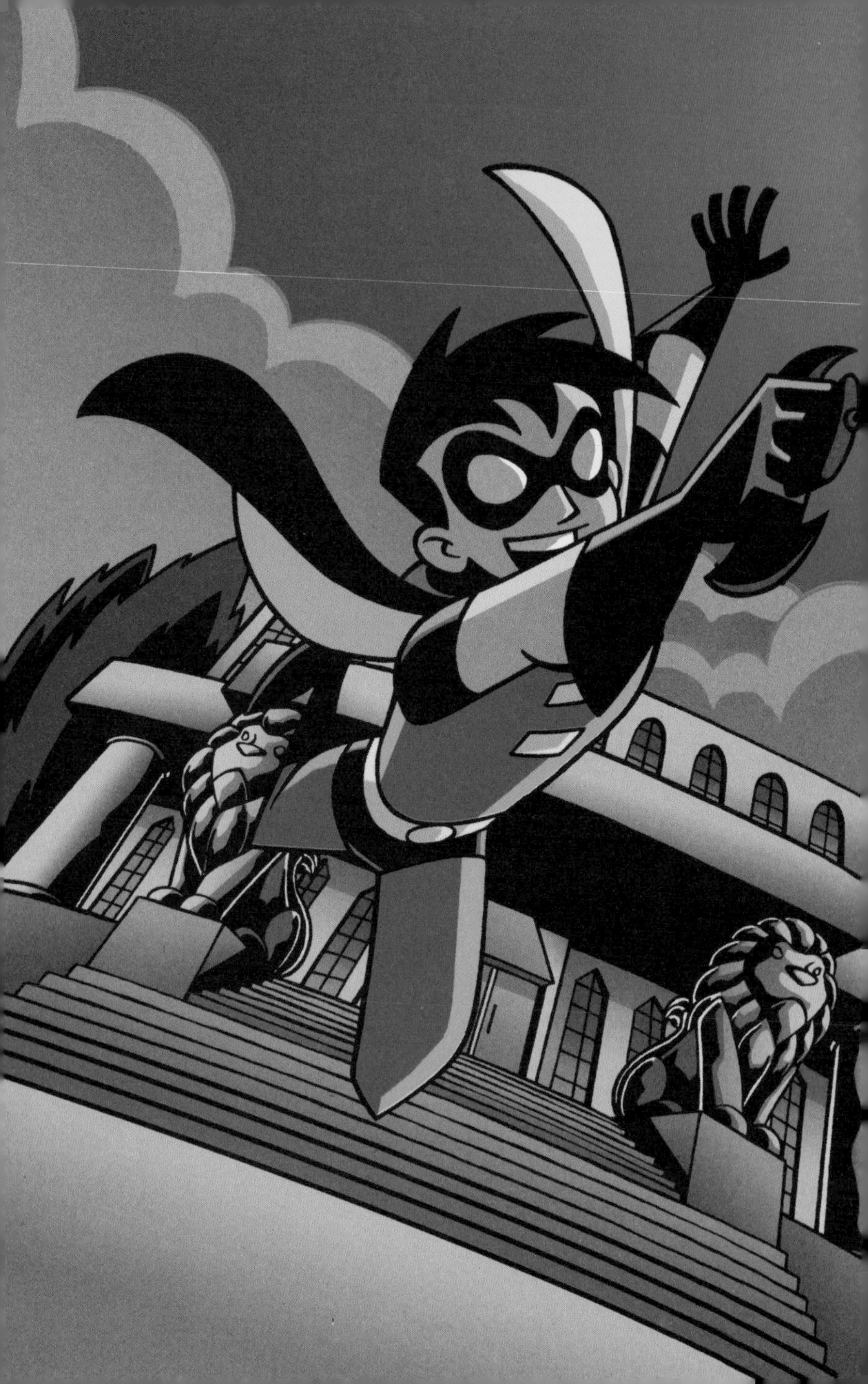

"Yahoo!" cried Robin. "This is way better than the high bar."

Robin hung onto the concrete wall like a lizard. He aimed his device at another building across an alley. ZING! The dart flew out and pulled Robin higher and further. Back and forth, the boy swung over the streets, hundreds of feet in the air. His target was the Bat-Signal.

It was good thing the teenager practiced gymnastics earlier that evening. And it was a good thing he had practiced blindfolded. He would need all his skills and focus this night as he swooped through the dark streets of the city.

# CHAPTER 5

# THE ROOF
# AT NIGHT

Miles away, on the top of the Spectrum Building, a strange searchlight was beaming its rays into the clouds.

A tall, thin figure dressed in green flipped off the searchlight's switch.

"GROOAANNNNNNN!" A second figure, dressed in black, moaned nearby.

"Something wrong, Batman?" asked the man in green. The huge searchlight had a lamp that was ten feet across. On the front of the lamp, a dark figure was chained.

His arms and cape were stretched out to either side. His legs and feet were chained together and fastened to the bottom of the lamp.

Batman was trapped. His own silhouette formed the bat outline whenever the cruel Riddler snapped the powerful beam back on.

"Don't you like my homemade version of your precious Bat-Signal?" asked the Riddler. "I couldn't do it without you, Batman."

The Riddler chuckled. "Yes, yes, I know it gets a little hot at times," he said. "But I'm just returning the favor — you're always making things too hot for me! Always foiling my plans! Solving my clever riddles too quickly!"

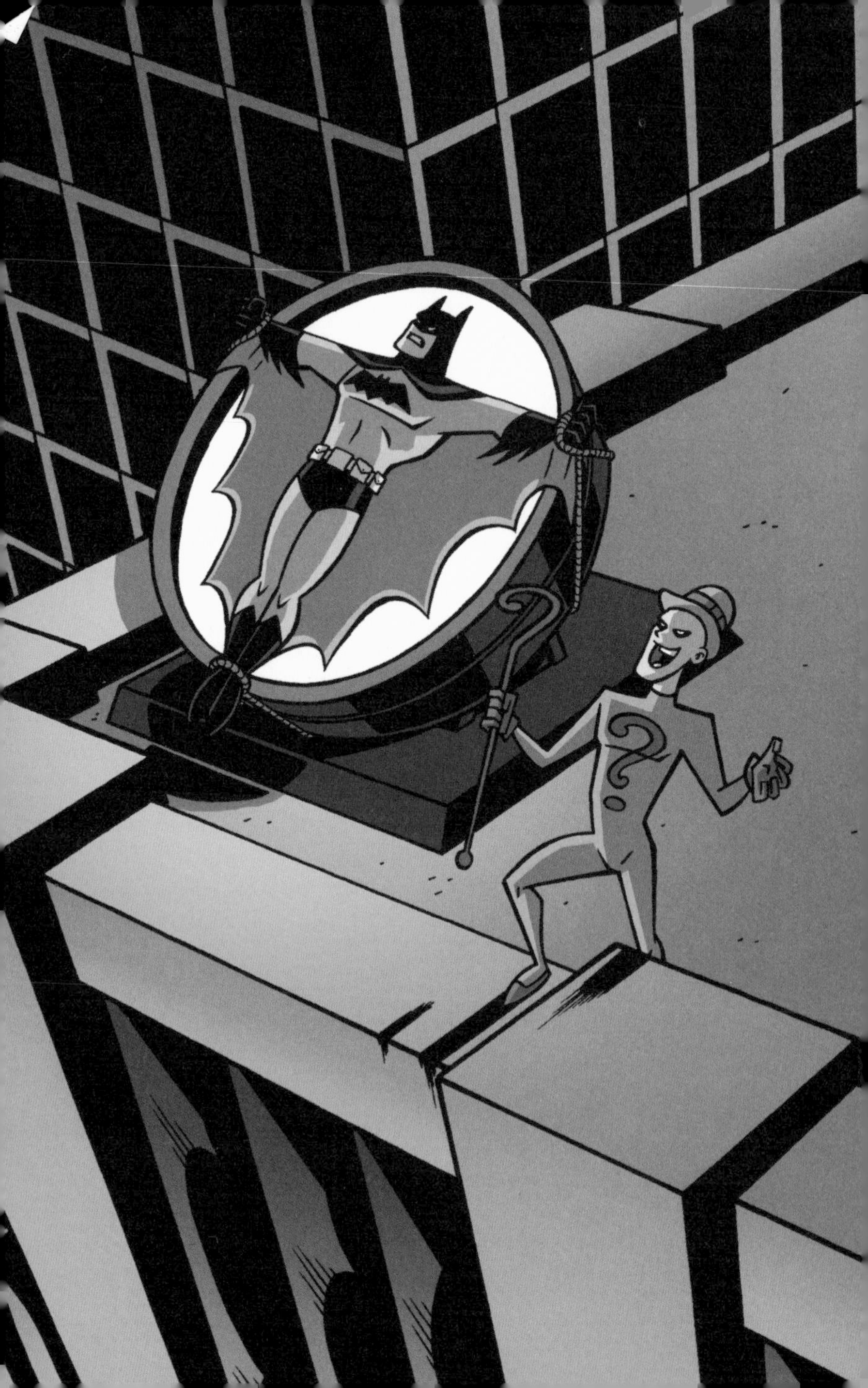

Batman groaned again. Whenever the Riddler had used the searchlight to trick Robin, the lamp had burned the backs of the Dark Knight's arms and legs. The pain was intense.

It was hard for him to concentrate. Even his special suit could not protect him from direct contact with the blazing lamp. Whenever the fake Bat-Signal was turned on, Batman felt as if his skin were on fire.

"Would you like some water, Batman?" said the Riddler. "You'll have some soon enough. This building is right next to Gotham River. And as soon as the sun comes up, I'm chucking you and this lamp over the side. You'll cool off plenty then."

"Ha! I think my riddles are keeping your young companion quite busy," the villain continued.

"Robin will be solving puzzle after puzzle until the sun comes up," said the Riddler. "But he'll never realize that his biggest riddle has been shining overhead all night long! Right over his nose! Ha ha ha!"

The Riddler walked up to the darkened searchlight. He stuck his wicked grin into the sweating face of his archenemy.

"You make the perfect signal, Batman," whispered the Riddler. "But no one would guess that it's you who are in trouble this time. I'm amazed you've been able to last this long against the heat."

The Riddler sniffed the air. "What's that wonderful aroma? Could it be Baked Crusader? I like mine well done."

A sharp metal object bounced against the rim of the searchlight.

The Riddler gasped. "What's that?" he cried. The metal object had cut through one of the chains holding Batman's left arm.

Another metal object swooshed through the air, missing Riddler's nose by an inch. It smashed against the metal searchlight and shattered the glass lens.

The Riddler recognized the metal object as it fell to the ground. A Batarang.

"Robin!" he screamed. The villain turned and saw a masked, red figure standing behind him. "But how did you find me?" he cried.

"You leave too many clues, Riddler," said Robin calmly. "That's always been your weakness."

The Riddler raised his question-mark cane. “Let’s see who’s really weak,” he said. He pushed a button and released a purple cloud of knockout gas.

“It won’t work this time, Riddler,” said Robin. “I was prepared for that trick, thanks to the video message you left behind.” The Boy Wonder placed a special gasmask against his mouth.

“Were you prepared for this?” asked the Riddler.

He flipped another switch on his cane. A bolt of electricity shot from the question mark’s tip.

Robin backflipped away from the bolt.

The Riddler laughed. “Don’t worry, kid,” he said. “Electrocution is a quick death. Much less painful than burning alive.”

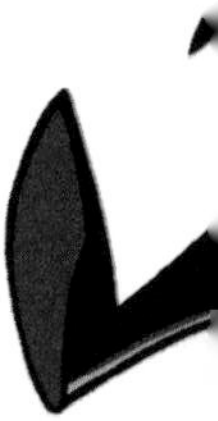

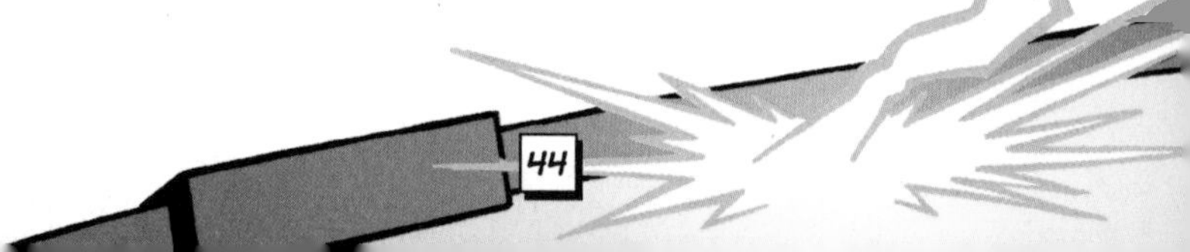

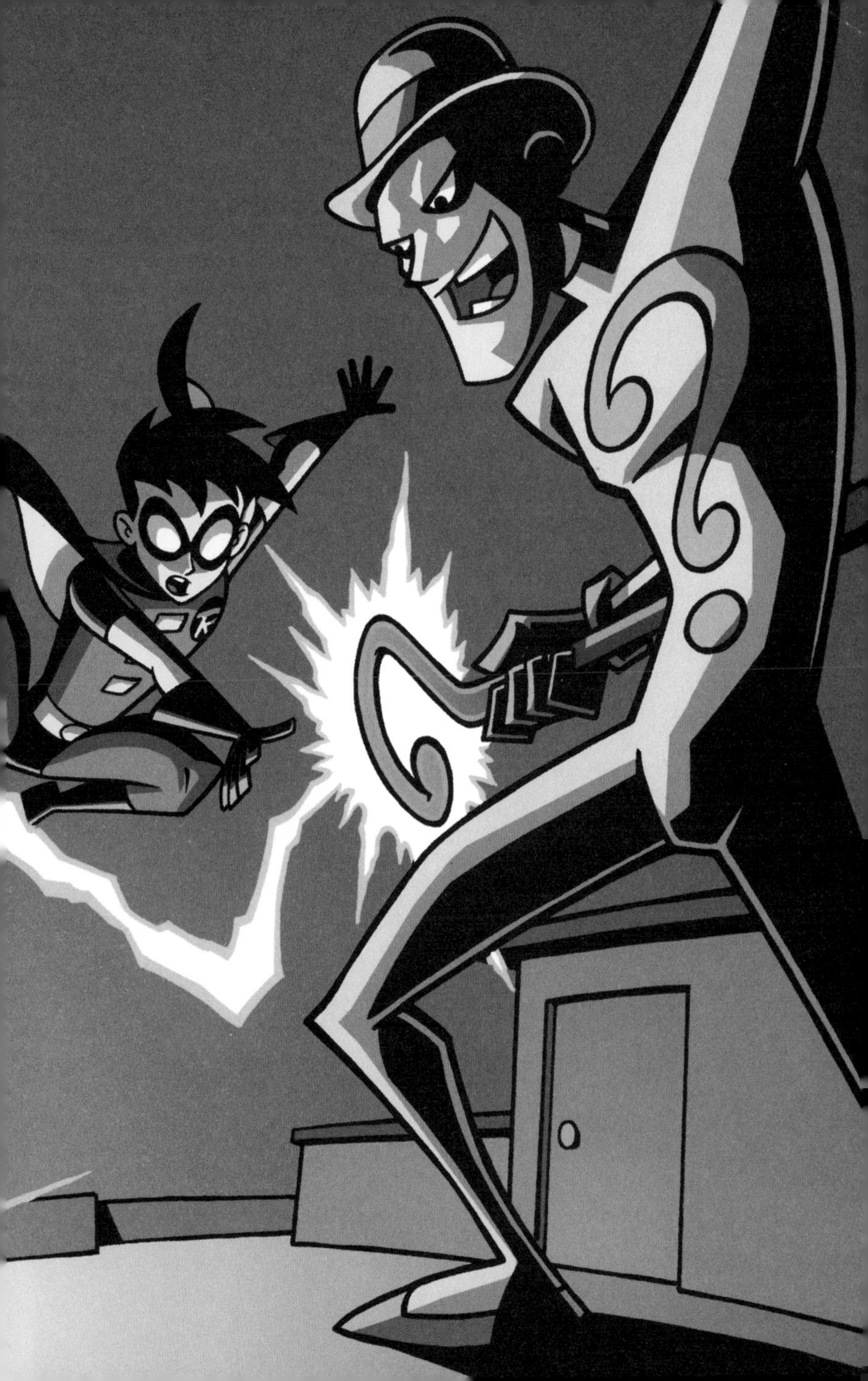

Another bolt flashed toward the young hero. He crouched low, letting the blast shoot past his head.

"That was way too close," said Robin.

He ran and ducked behind a metal air vent. A bolt from the Riddler hit the vent and sent it flying. Robin was hurled back and skidded along the surface of the roof.

"This game isn't fun anymore," said Robin. This time he ran straight toward the Riddler. The Boy Wonder pulled another weapon from his belt. Flash! The Batarang skimmed across the rooftop.

The Riddler fired. His deadly bolt hit the Batarang. But the metal weapon worked as a conductor of electricity. It sent the electric bolt back toward the Riddler's cane. The question mark crackled with energy.

**AAAAAHHH!** The villain screamed and dropped his weapon.

As the Riddler turned to run away, Robin pulled a bola rope from his belt and swung it through the air. It wrapped around the Riddler's feet, knocking him to the ground. Robin ran over and quickly cuffed the Riddler's hands behind his back.

Then Robin ran toward Batman. He used a small laser to cut through the remaining chains. Batman managed a weak smile.

"Robin," Batman began to say, and then the hero dropped to his knees.

"Careful, big guy," said Robin. "We'll get you back to the Batcave, pronto. We need to treat those burns. Don't worry. And I've already phoned Commissioner Gordon to come and pick up Riddler."

Robin helped Batman to his feet. He put his shoulder under Batman's right arm and guided him toward the building's stairwell. Before they reached the doorway, Robin turned and looked at the trussed-up Riddler.

"I've got a riddle for you, Riddler," said Robin. "When are you like a bottle of ink?"

The Riddler moaned. "Don't tell me — when we're both in the pen."

Robin smiled. "And you'll be in the pen for a long, long time," he said. Then he and Batman turned and greeted the morning sun as it touched the tips of the skyscrapers of Gotham City.

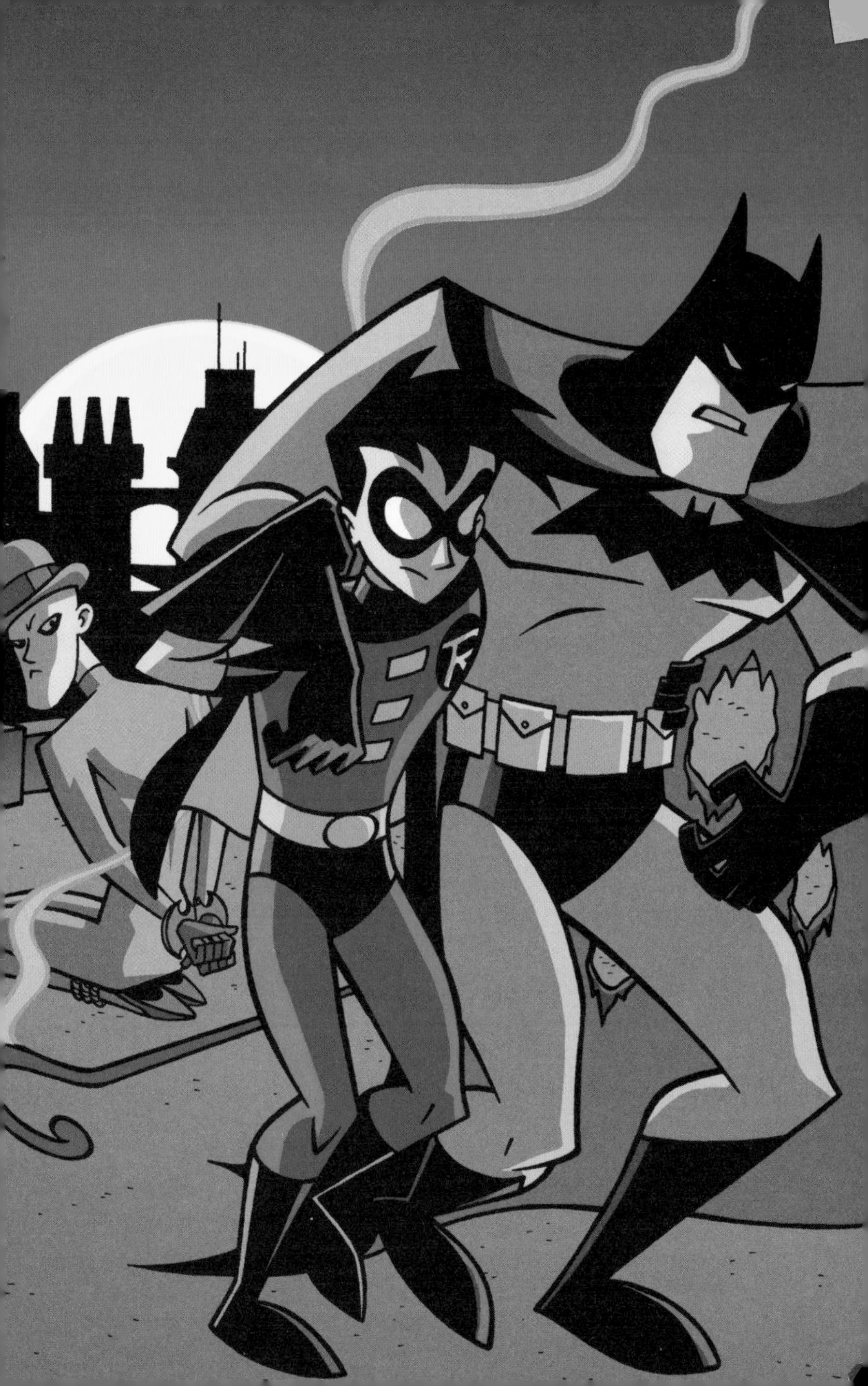

# Riddler, The

**REAL NAME:** Edward Nygma

**OCCUPATION:** Professional Criminal

**BASE:** Gotham City

**HEIGHT:**
6 feet 1 inch

**WEIGHT:**
183 pounds

**EYES:**
Blue

**HAIR:**
Black

Even as a little boy, Edward Nygma loved riddles and
puzzles. When he grew up, Nygma turned his passion
into a career. He became a video game designer and soon
invented a popular game called *Riddle of the Minotaur*.
The game sold millions of copies, but Nygma didn't
recieve a dime from the manufacturer. To get his revenge,
Nygma became the Riddler, a cryptic criminal who leaves
clues to his crimes.

# G.C.P.D. GOTHAM CITY POLICE DEPARTMENT

- The Riddler carries a cane shaped like a question mark. This weapon can deliver a shocking blast — the Riddler's answer to his toughest problems.

- The Riddler doesn't just want to break the law. He wants to outsmart Batman as well. Before every crime, the Riddler first sends a clue to Batman.

- The Riddler's real name suits him perfectly. Edward Nygma, or E. Nygma for short, sounds like the word "enigma," which means a mysterious person.

- Harry Houdini is one of the Riddler's greatest heroes. This real-life magician is famous for his stunts, tricks, and great escapes.

## CONFIDENTIAL

# BIOGRAPHIES

**Michael Dahl** is the author of more than 200 books for children and young adults. He has won the AEP Distinguished Achievement Award three times for his non-fiction. His Finnegan Zwake mystery series was shortlisted twice by the Anthony and Agatha awards. He has also written the *Library of Doom* series and the *Dragonblood* books. He is a featured speaker at conferences around the country on graphic novels and high-interest books for boys.

**Gregg Schigiel** is originally from South Florida. He knew he wanted to be a cartoonist since he was 11 years old. He's worked on projects featuring Batman, Spider-Man, SpongeBob SquarePants, and just about everything in between. Gregg currently lives and works in New York City.

**Lee Loughridge** has been working in comics for over 14 years. He currently lives in sunny California in a tent on the beach.

# GLOSSARY

**boasting** (BOHST-ing)—talking proudly about yourself in order to impress other people

**bola rope** (BOH-lah ROPE)—a weapon that has two round balls attached to a piece of rope. The bola is thrown at an enemy's feet, entangling him so that he can be captured.

**clenched** (KLENCHD)—held or squeezed something tightly

**confronting** (kuhn-FRUHNT-ing)—coming face to face with something

**device** (di-VISSE)—a piece of equipment that does a particular job

**mentor** (MEN-tawr)—a wise and trusted teacher

**shattered** (SHAT-erd)—broke into tiny pieces

**silhouette** (sil-oo-ET)—a faint outline or shadow of something

**torment** (tor-MENT)—to cause someone pain, worry, or frustration

**trussed** (TRUHSD)—tied or restrained

**villain** (VIL-uhn)—a wicked or evil person

# DISCUSSION QUESTIONS

1. In the story, Robin solves several riddles to save Batman. Which riddle did you find the most difficult and why? Were you able to solve any of the riddles before Robin?

2. Every super hero has special abilities or skills. Discuss some of Robin's abilities. How did they help him solve the case?

3. Billionaire Bruce Wayne is secretly Batman. Why do you think he keeps his identity a secret? If you were a super hero, would you tell anyone?

# WRITING PROMPTS

1. Riddles are questions that seem to make no sense but have clever answers. Try to write your own riddle. Then ask a friend to solve your puzzle.

2. Write your own Batman and Robin story. Who will the Caped Crusader and the Boy Wonder capture next time? You decide.

3. Batman relies on Robin for help in solving crimes. Describe someone that you rely on. What tasks do they help you with?

# MORE NEW BATMAN ADVENTURES!

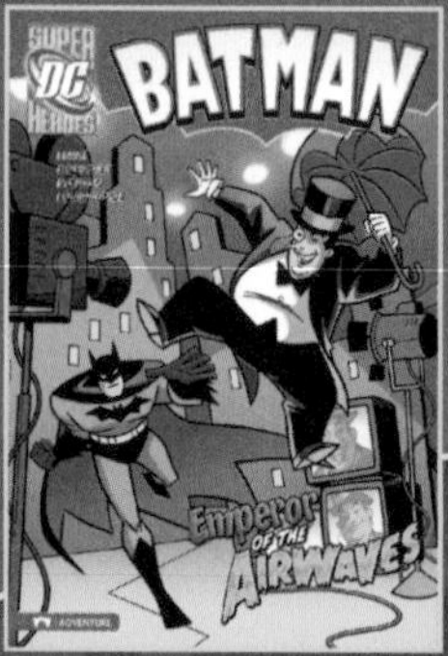
SUPER DC HEROES
BATMAN
Emperor of the Airwaves

EMPEROR OF THE AIRWAVES

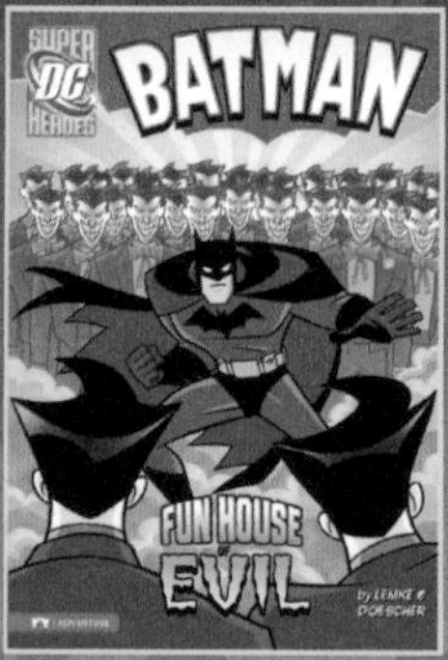
SUPER DC HEROES
BATMAN
FUN HOUSE OF EVIL
by LEMKE & DOESCHER

FUN HOUSE OF EVIL

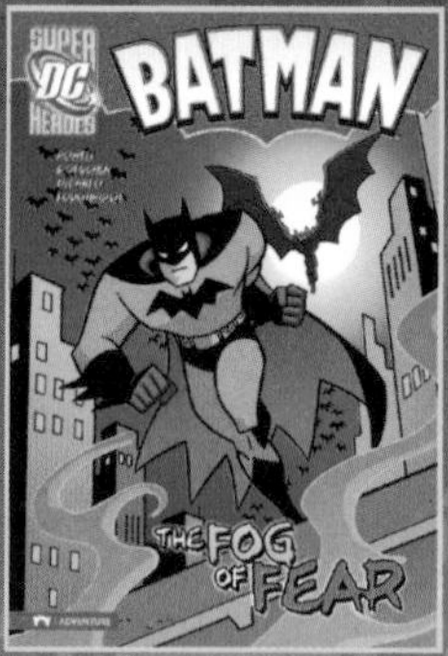
SUPER DC HEROES
BATMAN
THE FOG OF FEAR

THE FOG OF FEAR

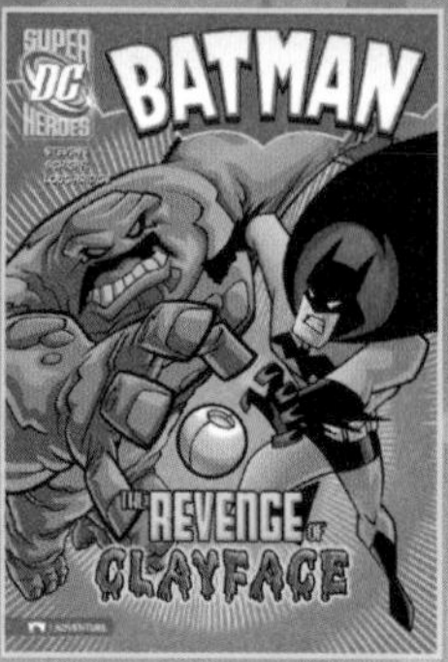
SUPER DC HEROES
BATMAN
THE REVENGE OF CLAYFACE

THE REVENGE OF CLAYFACE

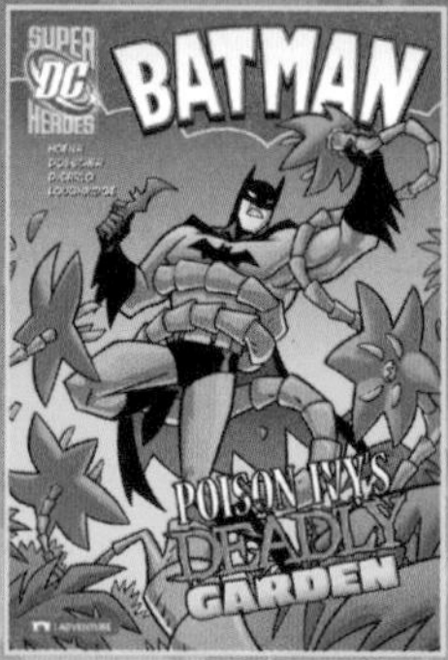
SUPER DC HEROES
BATMAN
POISON IVY'S DEADLY GARDEN

POISON IVY'S DEADLY GARDEN

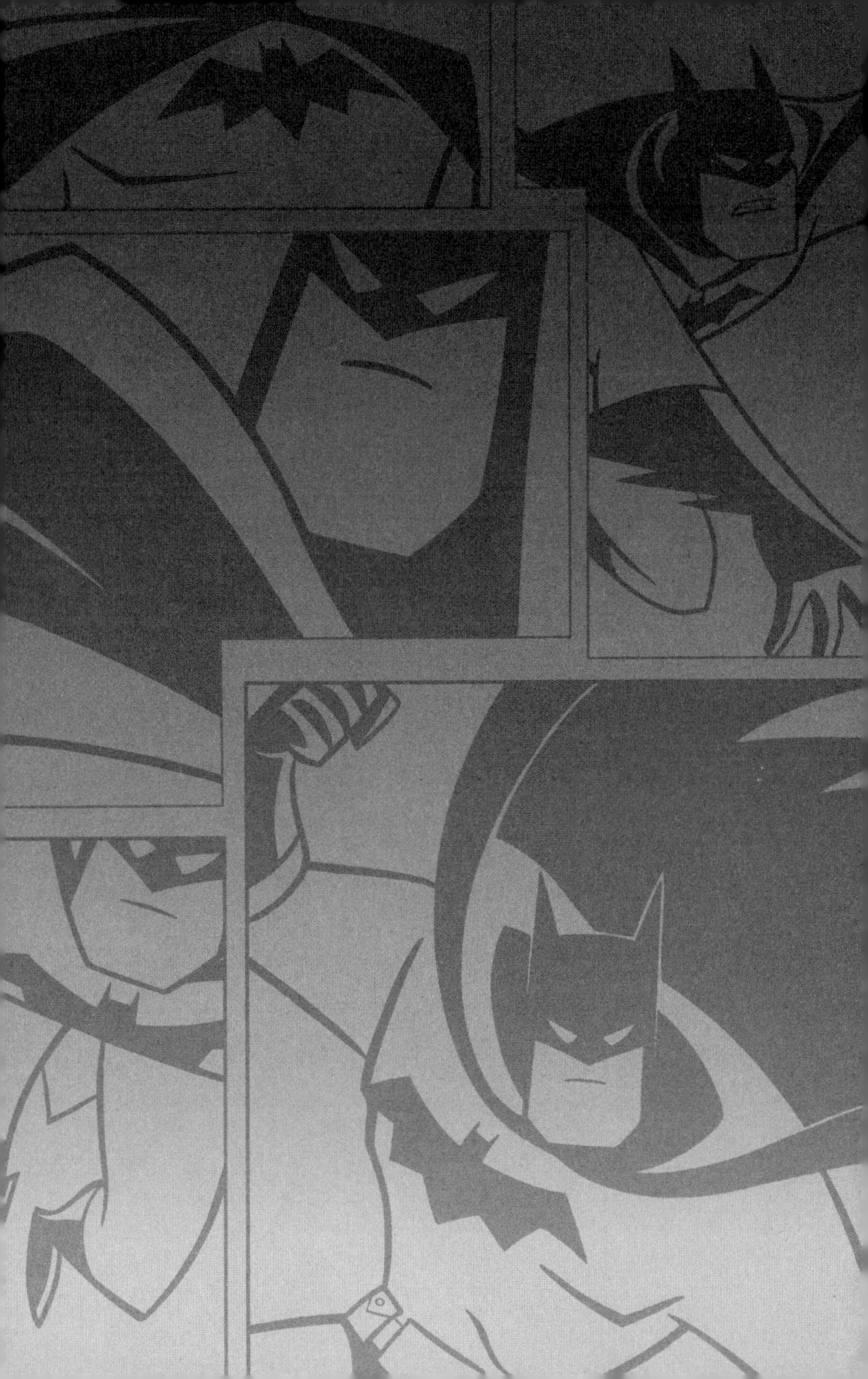

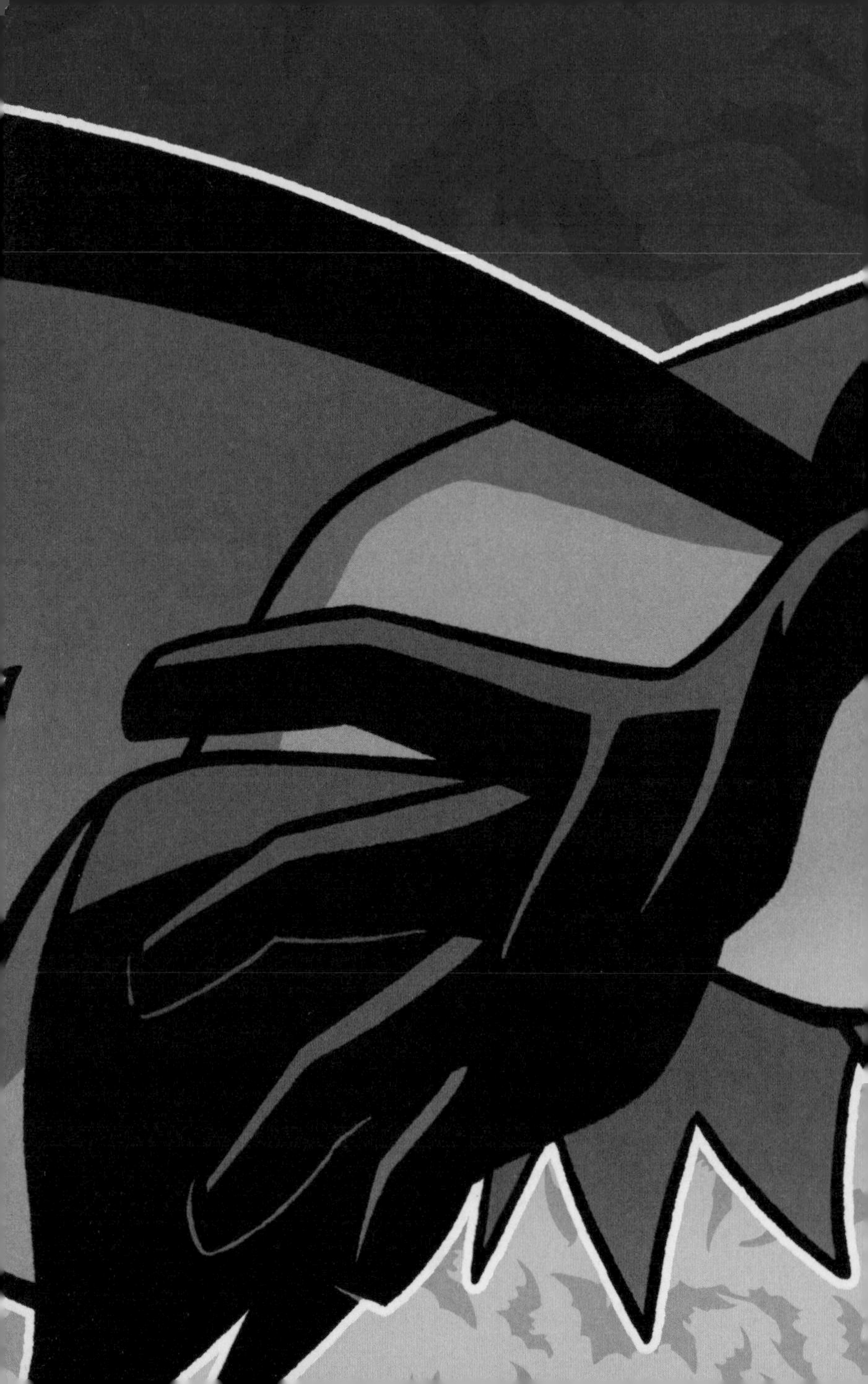

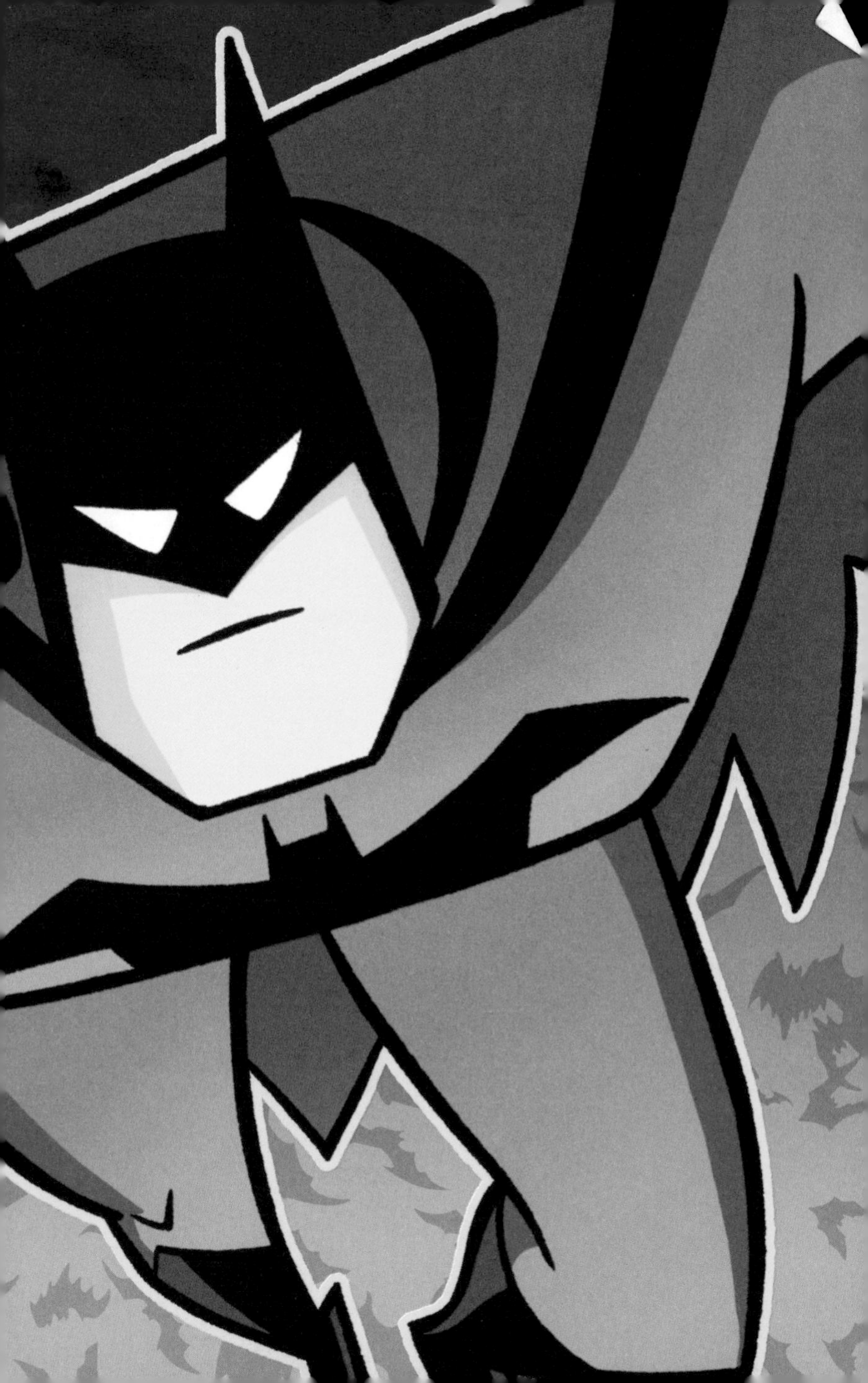